*This LADYBIRD TALE*
*belongs to*

............................................

# Peter
## and the Wolf

Retold by Kath Davies
with illustrations by Barbara Bongini

LADYBIRD TALES

ONCE UPON A TIME there was a boy called Peter, who lived with his grandfather in a little house beside a green meadow.

Grandfather knew of all kinds of dangers in the forest nearby and he tried to keep Peter safe. One day he said, "You must never leave the garden or go into the meadow alone, Peter. The hungry wolf might come out of the forest and eat you up."

Peter did not answer. He loved animals and birds, and he was sorry that the wolf was hungry. He wasn't at all afraid of it.

Early one morning, Peter opened the garden gate and went into the meadow. The wolf was not there.

High up in a tree sat a small bird. When Peter was near the tree, the bird said, "Hello, Peter! What are you doing here all alone?"

"Oh!" said Peter, looking up. "You made me jump! I'm out for a walk. Have you seen the wolf today?"

"No," said the bird. "I haven't seen him, and I don't want to see him." He went on, "That wolf's always hungry, he eats anything." He looked over Peter's shoulder. "There's a fine, fat duck," he said. "I'm sure the wolf would eat her. You'd better warn her about him."

Peter turned round to see a duck waddling up to him. She had followed him through the garden gate because she wanted to swim in the pond in the meadow.

"Hello, Peter," she said. "It's a fine day for a swim. I'm glad you left the garden gate open."

"Oh dear!" said Peter. "I hope Grandfather doesn't see it.
He told me to stay in the garden."

Peter said goodbye and went on by himself.

The small bird flew down to
the pond.

"Hey, duck!" he said. "Why did
you walk to the pond? It can't be
easy to walk on such flat, webbed
feet. Why didn't you fly like me?
What kind of bird are you if you
can't fly?"

The duck looked down at him.

"Fly?" she said. "Fly? Who wants
to fly? I can fly if I want to, but
I don't. I want to swim. And don't
be rude about my feet, because
webbed feet are made for
swimming." She turned her
back and dived into the pond.

"Come on in," she called.
"The water's lovely!"

The small bird jumped back quickly from the edge of the pond. "Who, me?" he twittered. "Swim? You must be joking. I don't swim." He fluttered his feathers nervously.

"Aha!" said the duck. "You mean you can't swim? What kind of a bird are you, then?"

The small bird hopped up and down in rage, the duck swam round and round the pool, and the argument went on. They were so busy arguing that they did not hear Peter come back. He stood near the pond in the long grass, and he watched them. They were very funny.

Suddenly, Peter saw a large, hungry cat crawling through the grass towards the small bird. The cat said to herself, "That bird is too busy shouting at the duck to notice me. I'll have him for my dinner."

She came closer, crouching low in the grass. Just as she was ready to jump, Peter shouted, "The cat, the cat! Oh! Look out, bird!"

The cat sprang forward, stretching her claws to catch the bird. But he flew straight up into a tree!

Peter looked up at the small bird. "You are very lucky," he said. "The cat almost had you for dinner!"

"Thanks, Peter!" said the bird.

Then Peter spoke to the cat. She was very angry, and she lashed her tail from side to side.

"Cat," said Peter, "you should be ashamed of yourself. Go away and don't chase the bird again. Go into the garden. I will give you some food when I get home."

The cat did not reply. She stalked away in a huff, her tail held high. When she reached the long grass, she sat down and began to wash herself. "See if I care," she thought. "Next time, I'll get that bird."

Not far away, Peter laughed, the bird sang and the duck quacked. They made a lot of noise because they were so happy.

After a while, Grandfather came out into the garden and saw that the gate was open. Grandfather was worried because he knew that Peter might be in danger. Then he heard the happy noises in the meadow, and he looked over the garden wall. He saw Peter, the duck and the small bird, and he was very angry.

"Peter!" he called. "Come here at once." Then he went out into the field to fetch Peter.

Peter heard his grandfather shouting. He stopped laughing, and ran towards him. "Come with me!" Grandfather ordered, and marched Peter back to the garden. He locked the gate behind them.

Grandfather said to Peter, "How many times have I told you not to leave the garden? Do you want the hungry wolf to eat you for his dinner?" Peter said nothing.

"Well?" said Grandfather. "Did you hear what I said?"

"Yes," muttered Peter. He was sorry, but he thought that Grandfather was making too much fuss.

Grandfather left Peter and took the gate key with him. He did not trust Peter to stay in the garden.

Peter was bored and unhappy in the garden. The small bird tried to help. He flew to a tree and sang to Peter, but Peter still didn't cheer up.

Meanwhile, the huge hungry wolf did come out of the forest. The small bird saw him first, and called in alarm to warn the duck.

The cat heard the bird's warning as well. She hissed in fright and climbed straight up the tree.

The duck was so frightened that she jumped right out of the pond. The wolf was coming – and he was the biggest wolf she had ever seen!

The wolf saw the duck and ran after
her. In a moment he caught her. He
opened his mouth – and swallowed
her in one gulp! She was gone.
A feather or two on the grass was
all that was left of the poor duck.

The small bird and the cat sat up
in the tree together, looking down
at the wolf. The bird had forgotten
to be afraid of the cat. And the cat
had forgotten about eating the bird!

The wolf was very pleased with the
fine dinner he had caught! He saw
the bird and the cat, and he thought,
"Ho, hum, do I see more dinner?"

Above him, the small bird and the
cat were too frightened to move.

Peter had seen what had happened.
"Silly duck," he sighed. "She would
have been safe if she'd stayed in
the pond."

Then he had an idea. He knew how
he could save the cat and the bird,
and he wasn't afraid of the wolf.

Peter found a long rope and ran out
into the garden with it, straight to
the garden wall. He tied the rope
carefully around his waist and
climbed the wall.

As soon as Peter was sitting safely
on top of the wall, he untied the rope
from his waist and began to make
a loop in one end of it.

From his high seat, Peter could see down into the meadow. He could see the wolf – and he could hear him growling. Peter could see the small bird and the cat sitting in the tree as well. The cat's tail was beating against the tree branch, but the bird was absolutely still. Peter knew that they were both very frightened.

The wolf was still prowling around the tree. Round and round he went. Sometimes he stopped to rest, and then he looked up at the cat and the bird in the branches above him. He growled horribly. The cat and the bird thought that he was growling at them, but he wasn't.

The wolf was beginning to feel quite ill. Inside him the duck was still alive and she was kicking his stomach hard. She was very cross, and she thought that if she could make the wolf hiccup, she might be able to jump out.

The wolf felt worse and worse.

Peter called out to the bird, "Fly round the wolf's head. Make him look at you. Then he won't see what I'm doing." The wolf was growling so loudly he couldn't hear what Peter was saying.

So the bird flew around the wolf's head. The wolf snapped at him, but he kept on flying round. Soon the wolf felt quite dizzy.

As the cat watched, she thought how brave the bird was, and she was glad after all that she hadn't eaten him for dinner.

Peter finished making the loop at the end of the rope. He tied one end of the rope to the tree, and he let the other end down carefully over the wolf.

By now the wolf was feeling very ill indeed, and he did not see Peter above him with the rope. Then suddenly, something pulled his tail very hard. It was Peter's rope! Now the wolf couldn't run away. The more he tried, the tighter the rope became around his tail.

All at once there was a noise in the forest. There were shouts and cries, and bangs and crashes. People were coming through the trees and bushes, blowing horns as they came. They were hunting the wolf.

When the hunters came out of the forest into the meadow, they saw the wolf beneath the tree, and they blew their horns to frighten him. Peter shouted, "Hey! Come over here. We've caught the wolf and he can't get away."

The hunters went up to the tree. They looked down at the wolf held fast at the end of Peter's rope. Then they looked up at Peter, the bird and the cat, and they were astonished.

"How did you manage to catch the wolf?" they asked Peter. So he told them what had happened. The hunters looked at the wolf, who was now lying down with his eyes closed.

"What are you going to do with him?" they asked. "He doesn't look terribly fierce."

The wolf opened his eyes and groaned.

"I don't think he's feeling very well," said Peter. "We're going to take him to the zoo. The zookeepers will look after him, and he won't be able to catch any more of my friends and eat them for his dinner."

Peter told the hunters about the duck. "Poor duck," they said.

Just then Grandfather came out into the garden and saw Peter on top of the garden wall. "What's going on now?" he called. "What are you doing on the wall?"

Then he saw the hunters and the wolf, and his face turned pale. When he went nearer, he saw that Peter was holding the rope, and the rope was holding the wolf. At that moment, Grandfather's face grew red with rage.

Before he could say one word, the hunters told him how Peter had caught the wolf. Now Grandfather didn't know whether to be proud of Peter or to be angry with him. He glared at his grandson, but there was a twinkle in his eye.

So they all set off for the zoo,
with Peter leading the procession.
After him came the hunters with
the wolf. The wolf was feeling
better, because the duck was having
a rest. She had stopped kicking
inside his stomach. Grandfather
followed the wolf, and the cat
walked beside him. The small bird
went with them.

The hunters blew their hunting
horns, and everyone came out to
see the wolf. They laughed and
cheered, then they ran to tell
their friends all about it.

The cat and the bird were happy
because the wolf was going away.
The hunters were happy because
Peter had caught the wolf.

Grandfather was happy because Peter was safe. Even the wolf was glad that he was going to a new home. He hoped the keepers would take away the pain in his stomach.

The duck was not too happy inside the wolf, but she knew that the zookeepers would soon rescue her. She quacked and quacked. All the people who heard her were puzzled, and kept looking around them. Wherever could she be?

Peter was happiest of all, because he knew that the wolf was never going to be hungry again!

# A History of
# Peter and the Wolf

The story of *Peter and the Wolf* was written as a musical composition for children by the Russian composer Sergei Prokofiev. The music is accompanied by a narrator, who tells the story to the audience while the orchestra plays the music.

Prokofiev wrote the story and music, intended to promote 'musical tastes in children from the first years of school', in just four days.

Since it was first performed in 1936, *Peter and the Wolf* has been used to teach millions of children about the way music can be used to tell a story.

In recordings, the role of narrator
has been played by some very
well-known people, including
Sir Sean Connery and David Bowie.
Disney produced an animated
version of the story in 1946.

This retelling was written
for Ladybird by Kath Davies
as part of the long-running series
of 'Well-Loved Tales'.

# Collect more fantastic

# LADYBIRD 🐞 TALES

### Little Red Riding Hood

9781409311126

### Goldilocks and the Three Bears

9781409311119

### Cinderella

9781409311072

### Jack and the Beanstalk

9781409311102

### The Gingerbread Man

9781409311096

### The Three Little Pigs

9781409311089

### The Three Billy Goats Gruff

9781409311065

### Pinocchio

9780723271062

### Puss in Boots

9781409311225

### Rapunzel

9781409311195

### Rumpelstiltskin

9781409311164

### The Elves and the Shoemaker

9781409311188

### Snow White and the Seven Dwarfs

9781409311171

### The Enormous Turnip

9781409311218

### The Magic Porridge Pot

9781409311201

### Sleeping Beauty

9781409311157

The Princess
and the Frog

9780718192556

Dick
Whittington

9780718192532

The
Big Pancake

9780718192549

Beauty
and the Beast

9780718192587

The Little
Red Hen

9780718192525

The Ugly
Duckling

9780718193133

The Princess
and the Pea

9780718192570

Chicken
Licken

9780718192563

The Emperor's
New Clothes

9780723271048

The Little
Mermaid

9780723271055

Hansel
and Gretel

9781409311133

Aladdin

9780723271079

Peter
and the Wolf

9780723294481

Snow White
and Rose Red

9780723294474

Endpapers taken from series 606d,
first published in 1964

A catalogue record for this book is available from the British Library

Published by Ladybird Books Ltd
80 Strand  London  WC2R 0RL
A Penguin Company

001

© Ladybird Books Ltd MMXV

LADYBIRD and the device of a Ladybird are trademarks of Ladybird Books Ltd

ISBN: 978-0-72329-448-1

Printed in China